D1124168

ISBN 0-86163-674-0 – cased

Copyright © 1993 Award Publications Limited

Published by Award Publications Limited,
Goodyear House, 52-56 Osnaburgh Street,
London NW1 3NS

Printed in Singapore

Ghost Stories

Illustrated by
JANE LAUNCHBURY

AWARD PUBLICATIONS LIMITED

Contents

The Flibbertigibbet

by Jane Launchbury.

Patrick took one look at his new house and didn't like what he saw. To start with, it certainly wasn't new, it was very old indeed and probably full of horrible ghosts. Inside, it was dark and dingy and smelled of mouldy dustbins. Patrick sighed and watched gloomily as the removal men carried his toys up the creaky stairs. He wished they hadn't had to move away from their nice modern house and all his friends.

"Come and look at your new room," called Patrick's mum. He peeped around the door very doubtfully. Boxes of his things were already scattered about the room, and in one corner there was a very big box. It was taller than Patrick's mum, and covered with a thick layer of dust. She brushed off some of the dust with her handkerchief and gave a gasp.

"It's a grandfather clock," she said.

Patrick glared at it. He had never seen such an ugly old thing before, and it didn't even have proper numbers on its dirty, smeared face.

"Perhaps we can get it to work again," said his mum. Patrick hoped not, he was sure it would be terribly noisy. He didn't really want the clock in his room, but it was far too heavy for his mum to move on her own, so there it stayed. Patrick pulled a face at the nasty old thing. He felt very fed up and lonely.

He had just found his favourite teddy bear when he noticed a strange sound. At first he thought it was one of his toys, but when he listened more carefully he realised that it was coming from the grandfather clock. Very quietly, it had started to tick. Patrick looked up at the old clock in surprise. It was rather a pleasant sort of tick. It almost seemed to be saying something.

"Tick Tock, I'm a very nice clock,
Tick Tock, Tick Tock."

Patrick clambered on to a box to have a closer look. As he wiped some more of the dust away from the clockface, he was sure he caught a glimpse of a face peeping through the glass.

"AAACHOO!" he sneezed, but when he looked again, all
he could see was the reflection of his own freckled face.
The clock ticked a little louder.

"*Tick Tock, turn the key in the lock,*
and let me out of the grandfather clock"

Patrick nearly fell off the box. This time the clock had
definitely spoken to him. Very carefully he turned
the key in the front of the clock. The door
swung open and out floated the strangest
little man. He had a long white beard
and wore a big dusty top hat, a
spotty bow tie, and a long coat
covered with colourful patches.

Patrick gasped, "W-what are you?" he stammered.

The little man slowly turned a somersault in the air, stretched his arms and legs, and made a deep bow.

"I'm not a WHAT, young man, I'm a flibbertigibbet, and I'm *very* pleased to meet you." Patrick just stood there with his mouth open in amazement, while the flibbertigibbet floated around the room peering into boxes and muttering to himself.

"Are you a ghost?" said Patrick, who had noticed that from certain angles the flibbertigibbet was almost transparent.

"Tick Tock Poppycock," said the flibbertigibbet. "Of course I'm a ghost, but I'm not a haunty, spooky sort of ghost, I don't really approve of that kind of thing." Then he sighed gloomily, "It's very lonely being a ghost. The people who lived here before were so frightened of me that they locked me in the clock and never came into the room. I'm not the sort of ghost that can float through locked doors."

Patrick felt very brave and proud of himself. He didn't think the flibbertigibbet was at all frightening, and within half an hour they were the best of friends. He told the flibbertigibbet all about himself, and quite forgot to think about how lonely and fed up he had been feeling. And the flibbertigibbet told him all sorts of amazing stories about the people who had lived in the house hundreds of years ago.

Then they unpacked Patrick's toys from their boxes. It took Patrick quite some time to explain about batteries and spaceships and things. You can miss out on a lot by being shut inside a grandfather clock for twenty years. The flibbertigibbet loved the radio-controlled cars and whizzed around the room on them.

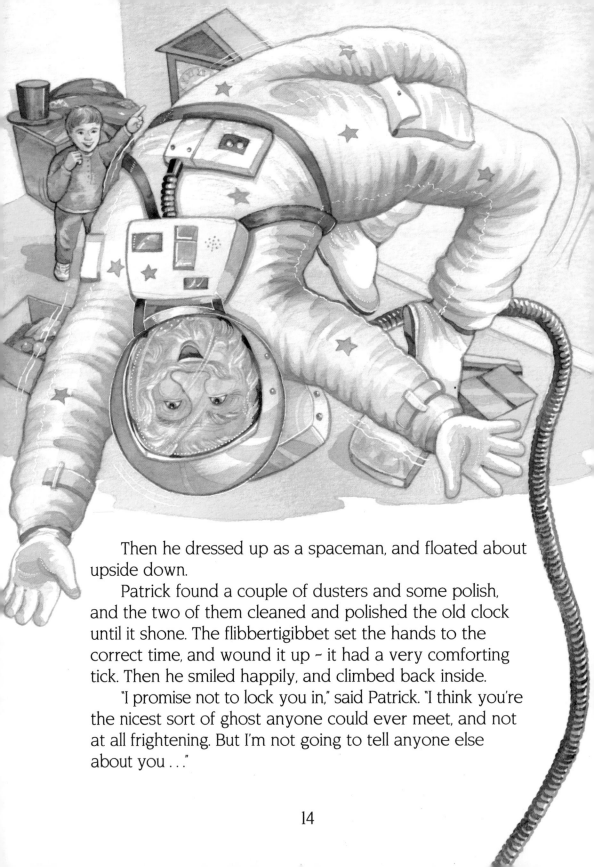

Then he dressed up as a spaceman, and floated about upside down.

Patrick found a couple of dusters and some polish, and the two of them cleaned and polished the old clock until it shone. The flibbertigibbet set the hands to the correct time, and wound it up ~ it had a very comforting tick. Then he smiled happily, and climbed back inside.

"I promise not to lock you in," said Patrick. "I think you're the nicest sort of ghost anyone could ever meet, and not at all frightening. But I'm not going to tell anyone else about you ..."

Just then Patrick's mum came into the room. She was amazed when she saw the shiny clock and heard it ticking.

"Please Mum, can I keep the clock in my room?" said Patrick.

"Of course you can dear," said his mum, "but I thought you didn't like it."

"I've changed my mind," said Patrick cheerfully. "And I think I'm really going to enjoy living here after all."

THE END

Haunt and Seek

by Maria Gordon

In the far distant past, Micklescrag was home to the brave monks of Foxhaven Abbey. Many were the frightened villagers who sheltered from the cruel Baron, and many were the tales of abbey ghosts sighted in its ruined towers and along the cliff paths . . ."

"No, stop, please Paul. I won't sleep if you read us any more." Jenny had said out loud what they all felt.

She and Paul, and their friends, Emma and Harry were
huddled in sleeping bags. They had been scaring sleep
away by swapping ghost stories, the torch throwing its
yellow beam spookily up on to their faces. Paul had
noticed his father's guide book which revealed that the
very spot where they were camped was thought to be
haunted.

"Ooh," shuddered Emma, "quickly, let's change the
subject!"

"Yes," agreed Jenny, "let's talk about tomorrow. What
shall we plan?"

"Spook spotting…   W-o-o-o-O-O-O-o-o-o !" wailed
Paul as the others tried to shut him up, half enjoying the
feeling of being scared.

"Mo, really. Lithen!" said Paul, trying to speak through Emma's hand which was covering his mouth and nose. Wriggling free, he continued. "I'm bored with the beach. We haven't really explored around here. Let's take the path through the ruins, play Hide and Seek and stuff."

"Haunt and Seek, you mean," said Harry, laughing as the girls threw their pillows at him.

"That's enough, kids," came a muffled response from the parents' tent. Hushed, the children settled down. But 'Haunt and Seek' stayed with them as a great idea for daylight chills and spills.

"Bagsy I'm first ghost!" announced Paul next morning. After some arguing the children agreed, mostly because Paul had persuaded his mum to lend them her cape. Normally Paul wouldn't be seen dead in his mother's cape. It was bad enough being with her when she wore something so unfashionable. But he had to admit that it made a perfect, not-so-tall, dark phantom outfit.

The game started with Emma, Harry and Jenny all finding separate hiding places, then Paul 'haunting' the ruins seeking prisoners. Paul and Jenny's mum and dad were spending the morning washing and cleaning by the two tents. They smiled to see the three friends disappear down the path through the overgrown, wooded abbey, followed shortly by Paul beginning his 'haunting'.

Swirling and swooping like an undersized Dracula, Paul soon spied Harry, huddled like a hedgehog under a lair of sticks and undergrowth. Paul crept closer, moaning eerily. With a final high pitched whine he tore away the pile of plants and branches. "Aargh! You big meanie! That was too scary!" yelled Harry, half laughing, as Paul hauled him off to a tower.

Emma was harder to find. She'd wriggled behind some bramble covered rocks. Well hidden, if a little prickled, she made the mistake of reading the Micklescrag guide book while she waited to be found. She gave herself away with a loud gasp as she read about one particular local ghost who dragged his head behind him. Unfortunately for her, Paul was right above, circling around doing his vampire impersonation.

"Gotcha!" he shouted, nothing like a good ghost.

Back at the tower, the three friends joined forces to 'haunt' Jenny. She had run further, right out to the abbey walls, which weaved a line of stony safety well away from the high Foxhaven cliffs. Where two walls met, a small, dark hollow had formed beneath them. Scrambling down, Jenny had squeezed into an archway almost completely below ground level. Totally unseen, she still had a good view of any approaching seekers.

Pleased with herself, Jenny began her lookout. She shivered, it seemed that a chill had settled despite the bright sunshine. But she soon forgot her chilliness as she peered out across the field with surprise.

'Oh no! It's Paul', she thought. 'He's made it up here already.' He was heading straight for her. She ducked down a little more, but it was no good. The hollow mustn't have been so well hidden after all. He didn't even bother to spook her, just waved for her to follow him.

Disappointed, she clambered out and looked up to see that Paul must have already gone back to the path. Dashing into the woods, she ran straight into him.

"Where have you been?" he asked.

"What do you mean?" said Jenny. "You know exactly…" A rumbling crash stopped her in her tracks. The ground trembled beneath their feet, and out in the walled field a cloud of dust billowed from Jenny's hollow.

"It's a tunnel!" reported their father, half an hour later.
Both adults had come running with Emma and Harry
when they heard the terrible noise which had echoed
through the woods. Shortly afterwards, a team of firemen
arrived to investigate and make the area safe. It was all
very exciting. Afterwards, one of the firemen had
explained that the dry summer had weakened the ground
until it collapsed.

"It's in the guide book!" said Emma, back at the tent. "The
monks led the villagers to safety. But not along the path,
they must have built a tunnel to lead out under the cliffs."

"Thank goodness you called me away just in time, Paul,"
said Jenny.

"But I didn't!" He protested. Everyone went quiet.

"But I saw you . . . the cape . . . haunting. Of course it was you."

"But it wasn't. Honest." It was obvious Paul was telling the truth.

"Oh! listen!" cried Emma. And from the guide book she read:

"Long after the monks left Micklescrag, many stories were told of a cloaked figure who would lead those lost in sea mist out of danger. There have been no recent sightings."

The tunnel was filled in and the ruins became safe again. And that was how they felt to Jenny, her family and her friends, who were somehow never frightened by the game of 'Haunt and Seek', which ended so strangely. They returned there many more times to camp, bringing with them the new Micklescrag guide book, which tells of the mysterious cloaked figure, but ends: 'There has been one recent sighting.'

THE END

The Highwayman

by Linda Jennings

One dark night in late November, the landlord of the Swan Inn was locking up when he thought he heard something. It was a sound he knew well and it filled him with dread.

"Quick! Fetch the lanterns, Molly," he shouted to his wife. "Hurry, perhaps we'll be in time to save them." The couple lit the lanterns, pushed open the heavy door, and ran, battling against the wind, down the lane leading to the misty wastelands of Witherby Marsh. Both heard the horses screaming. Then silence. Then only the sound of the sucking mud. The landlord turned to his wife.

"We're too late, Molly," he said.

Witherby Marsh was the haunt of Daniel Devlin, possibly the most dangerous and evil highwayman that ever roamed the roads of Britain at that time. Daniel Devlin would force stage-coaches to a halt, rob the passengers of all their valuables, and then drive them, together with their horses and carriage into the deadly waters of the marsh.

The landlord stooped at the edge of the marsh to pick something up. It was a blue silk scarf, patterned with silver threads. He handed it to his wife.

"Take it, my dear," he said sadly. "For I doubt if anyone will be claiming it."

"It was Daniel Devlin, then?" asked Molly.

"Who else?" said the landlord. They both stood, peering down the lane. The wind had dropped and a mist enveloped them. They heard, or thought they heard, the distant, muffled sound of a horse's hoofbeat.

"Too late to catch that scoundrel, too," sighed the landlord.

A year later, some customers were just leaving the Swan Inn, when a black-cloaked stranger galloped past. They caught a glimpse of a white, handsome face beneath an elegant tri-cornered hat.

"Don't go that way, sir," one man called after the fleeting figure. It's dangerous on the marsh at this time of year." A harsh, mocking laugh drifted back to them on the wind.

Daniel Devlin dismounted and positioned himself by the side of the road. It was a good spot, for a track led left, across the middle of the marsh and away from the Swan Inn. 'Easy to escape afterwards from the likes of that interfering landlord,' thought the highwayman. He had done it before, only last year. Daniel Devlin drew out his watch. The London coach was due in less than half an hour.

A sudden noise distracted him and he swung round. It seemed to be coming from the marsh. It didn't sound quite like an animal, nor like the reeds waving in the wind. It sounded like ~ like the rustle of silk from a woman's dress. But a woman? Here, on the marsh on her own at the dead of night? It didn't seem very likely. And then, as the moon came out from behind the scurrying clouds, the highwayman saw her. She stood by the side of the road, a blue silk scarf wound around her head. Daniel Devlin could see her dark curls escaping from the scarf, and blowing across her face. She was very, very beautiful.

Daniel Devlin never forgot a pretty face. Somewhere, he had seen this woman before. He had, he thought, asked her for a kiss. But there had been so many women, so many kisses . . .

Her hand was clutched to her cloak and he saw that she had a ring on her finger. The diamonds sparkled in the moonlight. The woman saw him looking at the ring and she held out her long, delicate hand to him.

Daniel liked the look of the lady and by the way she was smiling at him, he guessed that she liked him too. But he loved the diamond ring more. He reached for his holster and drew out his gun.

The lady did not flinch at the sight of the gun and for the first time she spoke.

"Take it," she said, "take my ring."

'Of course,' he thought, 'the lady is terrified - she's offering me her ring for her life.' But she did not look terrified.

"I have no need for it," she continued. "I have more jewels at home than I can count." She drew the ring from her finger, and handed it to Daniel Devlin. And while he stood looking at it in astonishment, she turned and began to walk away from him. She took the path to the left of him, his escape route. The highwayman slipped the ring into his pocket, and hesitated. The London coach would soon be here, with all its riches. But the lady was walking away towards a house that contained countless jewels. How could he reisit that - and perhaps a kiss too? Daniel Devlin tied his horse to a tree, and began to follow the lady down the track on foot.

It was difficult to keep
her in sight, as the mist
swirled around her. It grew
thicker and thicker, so that the
highwayman could barely see the
path in front of him. Then she
suddenly appeared again. He saw her face
clearly in the moonlight, and she was smiling back
at him.

'*She did not smile the last time,*' he remembered.
'*She spat in my face.*'

He reached into his pocket to feel for the ring she
had given him. It was not there. It *must* be there, he
thought, he had put it in his left pocket. It was a deep
pocket, with no hole, so the ring couldn't have fallen out.

No time to worry about the ring. No time to wonder
where he had met the lady before. The track was growing
narrower and rougher. Where was the lady now? He
could see nothing through the mist, but he could still hear
the sound of her rustling skirts. Thinking only of her
countless jewels, he turned to follow her.

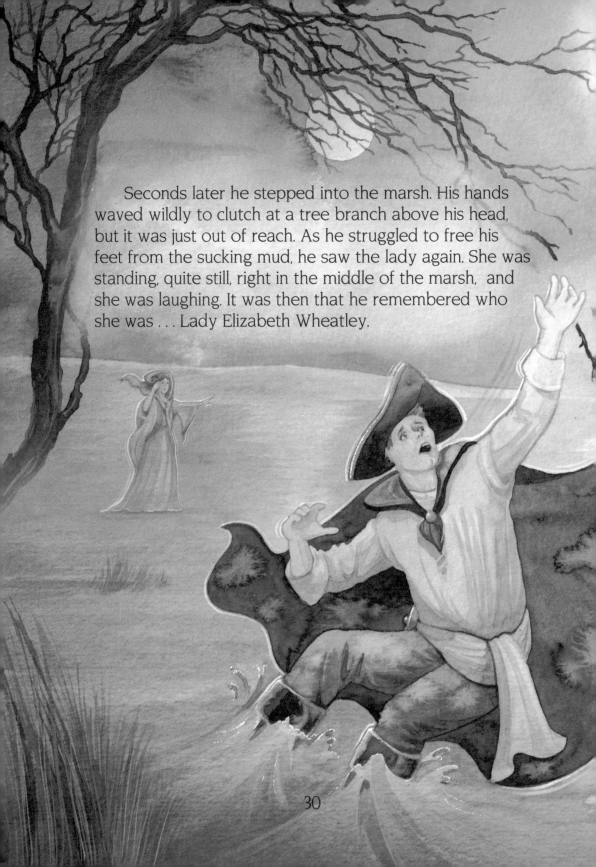

Seconds later he stepped into the marsh. His hands waved wildly to clutch at a tree branch above his head, but it was just out of reach. As he struggled to free his feet from the sucking mud, he saw the lady again. She was standing, quite still, right in the middle of the marsh, and she was laughing. It was then that he remembered who she was . . . Lady Elizabeth Wheatley.

A year ago, to the very night, Daniel had robbed her coach. He remembered now, too late, how he had roughly clasped her slender waist and demanded a kiss. And how she had spat in his face. Then he had pushed her back into the coach and at the point of his gun, had forced the coachman to drive into the deadly waters of Witherby Marsh.

As first Daniel's feet, then his legs were sucked down into the marsh, he started to scream. His screams echoed and re-echoed around the marsh.

At the Swan Inn, the landlord stood for a moment at the open door.

"I thought I heard a scream, Molly," he said. "Out there on the marsh."

"I can't hear anything now," said Molly, and the couple went back inside, and bolted the big, heavy door.

THE END

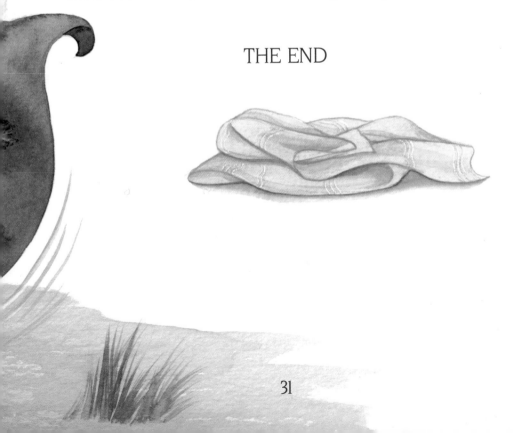

Haunting at Crickleback Way

by Maria Gordon

Once upon a time, at number thirteen, Crickleback Way, lived two children with a very important question on their minds.

"Do you think this house is haunted?" Tom and Mandy asked their mum. She clanked her mop bucket wearily on the floor and said sharply, "Now you know there's no such thing as ghosts. Off you go and play. Let me get on!" That put an end to any conversation. Disappointed, the children stalked upstairs. Little did they know that this would be a day they would never forget.

Bored, Tom and Mandy began rearranging their bedroom furniture. Mandy's wardrobe was moving nicely, when a rasping creak from the front gate drew them to the window facing the garden. It was there that they saw him.

Hunched and hollow eyed, wearing a long, black overcoat, a stranger paced up and down, jangling a huge set of keys from hands clasped behind his back.

"Must be a burglar!" said Mandy. Bravely, Tom knocked on the window to scare him away. The eerie figure below paid no attention.

The two children ran to find their mum. They got only as far as the hall. Hiding behind the stairs they watched as a key turned in the lock, a shaft of sunlight broke the gloom and, slow and mysterious, the man stepped inside. Mandy and Tom stepped back.

"Ouch!" they called out as they banged their heads.

"Look! He hasn't heard us," Mandy whispered. The stranger stood staring coldly just ten feet away, moaning and muttering miserably. "He can't hear and I bet ..." cried Mandy suddenly leaping out from their hiding place, "... he can't see us!" She was right. Tom joined her to stand grinning and waving right in front of the intruder. Then, at the same time, they both stretched out their arms just far enough to reach the man's sleeve and feel ... nothing! Their hands went straight through!

"He's a ghost!" gasped Tom in delight. For the next ten minutes the children followed their ghost around the house, even taking it in turns to leap right through him! Then, as strangely and spookily as he'd come, he left, sighing grimly and shaking his keys.

Tom and Mandy's mum and dad didn't believe a word of it.

"Sounds as if you've got a touch of the sun. You know you shouldn't play out in it too long!" grumbled their dad. Then it was bedtime.

"He was a ghost, I'm sure," said Mandy.

"I know," replied Tom.

"What a funny black coat . . . and those keys! And wasn't he warm?" Mandy sighed happily, glancing out at the bright sunshine. And, with the rest of her family, she disappeared, just as all real ghosts do!

"I spent ages up at Crickleback Way," moaned Mr. Sproggett. "Quiet as a mouse up there. Not a soul to be seen!" He hung up his long, black overcoat, walked into his office, and tossed his large, jangling keyring on to his desk.

"Didn't Mr. and Mrs. Smith turn up then?" asked his secretary. "You know," she continued, "I think we'll have trouble selling that house. A lot of people think it's haunted . . ."

THE END

SPROGGETT & SPLUDGE

FOR SALE

Tel: Haunton 653

Butterfingers

by Jane Launchbury

Juliet's mother gave a loud shriek, and dropped the saucepan she was holding. Frozen peas bounced all over the kitchen floor!

"Whatever's the matter, mum?" asked Juliet. Her mum stared around the room with an open mouth, then simply shook her head and began to scoop up the peas.

"Nothing dear," she said. How could she even start to explain to Juliet that she'd just seen her husband's spectacles float across the kitchen ... all by themselves, through thin air ... it was impossible!

It's a shame she didn't mention it, because Juliet could have *tried* to explain everything ... It had all started a month or so before, when some strange things happened in the Hudson household.

Several times, everyone was woken in the night by a loud crash, and in the morning when they went downstairs, they found something smashed to pieces on the floor. Juliet's mum blamed the two cats, but her big brother Danny said it was quite definitely a poltergeist. He'd seen a film about one once, a sort of ghastly ghost that threw things about and haunted people.

"It was dead scary," he said, and wailed "Oooooooh Waaaaaah!" until he got on everyone's nerves.

Juliet tried not to think about it too much, but she knew it couldn't have been the cats every time. There was one occasion when the best blue vase had been broken in the night. She'd been in charge of drying-up and putting-away after dinner, and she knew she'd locked the door to the china cupboard with its little silver key. The cats couldn't possibly have unlocked the cupboard and taken out the vase. A tiny shiver ran down her spine . . . what if Danny was right?

That night, Juliet was woken up by a thump and a
bump beside her bed.

"Go away, Danny," she grumbled sleepily, and turned
over.

"Butterfingers!" hissed a voice in a loud whisper.

Puzzled, Juliet opened her eyes, no one had called her
by that nickname for years. She was just in time to see a
blur that looked very like her model aeroplane, fly across
the room, and crash-land in the open sock drawer.

"Double butterfingers! You're *useless!*" hissed the same voice. "I'm not playing with you any more." Juliet sat up with a start, her heart beating very fast.

The street lamp outside cast a soft orange glow into her room, and she peered into the gloom. Everything was very blurred, so she reached for her glasses. She gave a little gasp when she saw that it had indeed been her model aeroplane flying across the room. There was its tail-fin sticking out from the sock drawer.

"Oh, drat," came a soft voice, "where on earth did it go?" Juliet froze ... Danny must have been right, it was a poltergeist! A horrible invisible ghost come to haunt her!

"Oooh woe, whatever shall I doooo, it's just not fair" wailed the invisible voice, then it began to snuffle and snivel, and soon it was sobbing uncontrollably. Juliet swallowed hard and thought for a moment. The voice hadn't really sounded that scary, and now its owner was crying. Quite definitely, whoever it belonged to seemed even more scared than she was.

Juliet cleared her throat, "Wh-h-oo a-are y-y-ooo", she managed to stammer, sounding rather like a ghost herself. The sobbing stopped, and there was a long pause.

"P-p-please d-don't be scared, I c-couldn't bear it if you were s-s-scared," stammered the gentle, ghostly voice. Juliet bit her lip hard.

"I'm not", she lied, "well maybe just a little bit . . . Are you a p-p-poltergeist?"

There, she'd said it, and now she'd know the worst.

"Of course I'm not a poltergeist," said the voice, sounding rather disgruntled. "I'm just an ordinary, common or garden ghost, the sort that every good home has. It's just that people keep *thinking* I'm a nasty poltergeist because I can't catch, and I keep dropping things. Everywhere I go, somebody has me exorcised - that means I get sent away, and I can't go back again. I only moved into your home five weeks ago, and now I'll have to leave. Nobody wants to live with a butterfingered ghost around. Ooooooh, woe is me . . ." The sobbing began again.

Juliet tried to take in all this information.

"Why do you need to throw things around anyway?" she said.

"It's something that's expected of all good ghosts," said the ghost. "There's not a lot else for us to do, so it's become an essential feature of ghostliness. Part of the skill is to be able to haunt anywhere without any living person ever knowing about it. Most people have ghosts living with them, and never ever find out. But when I play with the other ghosts, I'm no good at the catching bit, so things get dropped and broken. The other ghosts get fed up of playing with me. And then the people who live there find out about us and get us *all* sent away. Oooooh wooooah, it's so unfair."

Juliet thought hard, and a little smile came to her lips. She'd had that same problem with catching things until the optician had come to her school, done a sight test, and she'd been given a pair of spectacles. Before then, *she'd* been called 'Butterfingers' too! Carefully, she took off her spectacles and gingerly held them out to the ghost.

"Try wearing these," she said.

Gently, the invisible ghost lifted the glasses, and Juliet saw them float through the air.

"Wow … I can see!" gasped the ghost. Of course, Juliet couldn't see the ghost at all, but she could just about see her glasses.

They floated all around the room, while the ghost explored the new world it could see properly. Juliet picked up her teddy-bear, and tossed it toward the floating spectacles. It stopped, and appeared to hover in mid-air.

"Hooray!" said Juliet, "now you can see, you can catch! So whenever I'm asleep, you can borrow my glasses - as long as you're careful with them and always give them back when I wake up." The ghost was delighted, and Juliet was pleased too. She was a girl who liked to be helpful, and besides which, it meant that there would be no more crashes in the middle of the night.

What she hadn't thought about, however, was that her dad wore glasses too, and he sometimes had a little snooze in front of the television when he came home from work. So now you can guess what had happened that teatime when Juliet's mum saw something very strange indeed in the kitchen . . .

THE END

43

Ghost Train

by Linda Jennings

"**B**ut I can't see you on to the train," said Mum, who had an important meeting at work.

"Don't worry," said Mike. "We're quite old enough to know which train to catch." Mike and Diana were going to stay with their aunt and uncle in Polchester. Mum had looked up the train timetable and told Uncle Sam what time the two children would be arriving.

"Remember, it's the 10.42, direct to Polchester," said Mum, "don't get on any other train." Mike, who was a year older than Diana, took a careful note of the train time and felt very grown up.

Now, here they both were, with their bags, standing on the station platform. They didn't have long to wait.

"There!" said Diana, "this is the one. The electronic indicator flashed the destination: '*Polchester*' with the time beside it. The train drew in, and Mike and Diana climbed on board. As it pulled out, they noticed lots of people still standing on the platform.

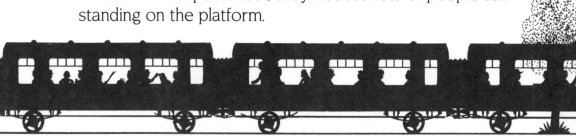

"Funny," said Mike, "I'd have thought everyone would have wanted to go to Polchester. That old lady standing over there said she would, I heard her."

"Don't panic," said Diana, "we're on the right train, we saw the indicator, remember." The two children sat down. Opposite them a man wearing a hat was reading a newspaper, and in a corner there was a woman nursing a tiny baby. Diana and Mike peered at the man's newspaper and tried to work out some of the answers to the crossword on the back. Mike soon lost interest, and yawning, he stared out of the window. Suddenly he sat up straight.

"Diana!" he cried, "we're on the wrong train! We should be going past the end of our road now, and it's not there!" Diana looked out of the window too.

"That's odd," she said. "The housing estate's not there, but the lake is - look!"

"It must be another lake," said Mike, "houses and roads don't just disappear!" The train whizzed through a station - Berrytown.

Diana looked at Mike with wide eyes. "That *is* the next station after ours, Mike, we *must* be on the right train." Both children felt a little scared. Something very strange was happening. As they looked around the carriage they noticed other odd things. There was a leather strap to open the window, and brown, faded looking photographs were framed under each rack.

"Perhaps we've caught a special, vintage train by mistake," said Mike. He breathed a sigh of relief. "Yes, that must be the answer."

"Hmmm . . . vintage trains don't make roads and houses disappear!" retorted Diana. She leaned over to speak to the man with the newspaper. "Excuse me," she began, "I wonder if . . ." but the man took no notice of her whatsoever. "How rude," she sniffed.

Someone opened the sliding door from the corridor.

"Tickets, please," said the inspector.

Mike took their two tickets and held them out, but the inspector completely ignored him. The man behind the newspaper thrust out a hand with a ticket in it, without even bothering to lower his paper.

"Thank you, sir," said the inspector. "Thank you madam," he said when the woman with the baby handed him her ticket.

Diana nudged Mike.

"Did you see those tickets? They didn't look like normal ones. They were small and green, like little bits of cardboard. It's all very odd if you ask me. That inspector didn't even seem to see us. And look, we've just passed Siddlecombe Junction, and we should be able to see the motorway – but we can't."

Diana was studying the back of man's newspaper again. Just at the top, under the title of the paper was a date, '15th June 1948,' she read. She grabbed Mike by the arm.

"Mike! We're in a time slip! We're travelling on a train that went this way over forty years ago!"

Mike didn't want to believe that, because he was a practical sort of boy, but the date rang a bell . . .

Both children sat quietly, their hearts thudding, trying to remember what was significant about the 15th June 1948.

Diana suddenly went very pale.

"Mike", she said, in a low voice, "I remember now. When our class did a history project, we found out about a terrible train crash on this line. I remember reading about it at the local library. A train travelling to Polchester crashed into the back of another one just outside Polchester station . . . Most of the passengers were killed or badly injured . . ." Mike leapt to his feet.

"Pull the communication cord!" he shouted, "we've got to get out!"

Diana was crying, "It's no use, can't you see? We don't really exist here at all. That man can't see us, nor can the ticket inspector. If we pulled the cord, it probably wouldn't make any difference."

"Try it," said Mike in desperation.

Diana stood on the seat and pulled the communication cord. Nothing happened. The train raced on. The man with the newspaper turned a page and didn't look up. The woman with the baby carried on rocking it gently.

Diana tried to open the window. She yanked hard on the leather strap, and the window flew wide open. A great

gust of wind blew in, and woke the baby, who started crying loudly. The man lowered his newspaper, sighed very crossly and glared at the mother. The baby screamed louder than ever, and the man carried on glaring at it. Embarrassed, the woman got up, apologised to the man, and said that she would move to another compartment with the baby.

The train raced onwards.

"Perhaps we can jump off," said Mike, peering out of the window, "then we could run to the nearest signalbox and stop the train. We could avoid a huge tragedy." Diana stared at her brother.

"You can't change the past," she said. It's all over and done with ~ we can't stop anything." Mike started to shiver.

"But if we can't change it, and we can't get off the train . . ."

Diana shook her head, "I don't know, " she said, "I don't know what will happen." The children couldn't sit still, they got up and walked down the corridor, peering into compartments. There were people in all of them, reading, sleeping, talking, staring out of windows, all oblivious of their fate.

"I can't bear it," said Mike.

"Not everyone was killed," said Diana, "there were some survivors."

Mike went very quiet, he had read a story once where a girl had been trapped in another time, and had died before she had been able to get back to her own time. It was just a story, but . . .

The train whistled through Stonestown station, the stop just before Polchester. Then, miraculously, it began to slow down.

"Jump out!" cried Mike, flinging open the door.

They flew through the air, down, down on to the grassy bank beside the track. The train jolted, picked up speed, and was away round the bend, leaving Mike and Diana dazed on the ground, staring after it.

"Now what?" said Diana, "we're off the train, but still back in that time ~ " she broke off . . .

Two things happened at once. From away down the line came a sickening, crunching, crash, but this was immediately drowned by the roar of a supersonic plane roaring low overhead. The children instinctively covered their ears and shut their eyes.

"I feel funny, sort of dizzy," said Diana. Mike did too, but something else had occurred to him . . .

"They didn't have supersonic planes in those days," he mumbled, "Ugh, my head's spinning, I can't think straight."

"Mine too," said Diana . . .

One minute the two children were standing beside the track, not two minutes outside Polchester, and the next they were standing on their own, home station.

The indicator was flashing '*Polchester*, 10.42.'

"How do we know," said Diana in a small voice, "I mean ~ how do we *know* that *this* train's the right one?"

But as the big, bright, Inter~city train pulled in, all the other passengers on the platform got on. Mike and Diana followed them.

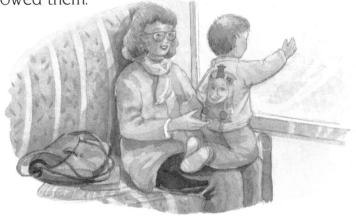

They sat opposite a woman with a little boy, who peered eagerly out of the window.

"He loves trains," said the woman to Mike and Diana, "which is more than I do, I can tell you. Nearly killed by a crash, I was, on this very line in 1948. I was a tiny baby then of course. Apparently a sudden draught woke me up and I started screaming the place down. If my poor old mum hadn't walked all down the train looking for an empty compartment, we'd have both been smashed to smithereens! Terrible crash it was, but of course, you wouldn't remember it, would you?"

THE END

Seeker
of the
Ring

by Maria Gordon

There was a full moon against the dark September sky, and a strange stillness over Scarduggen Castle. One owl's blink and a rabbit's twitch caught danger in the air and wildlife scurried far from the ancient walls. From the tower came the sound of mocking laughter carried softly on the breeze. A black cat stretched, flexed its claws and glared down from the tower. The ghost of Baron Scarduggen was risen once more.

Safe within strong, stone cottage walls, James Purbeck thought nothing of Scarduggen Castle, high on the hilltop above the village. Digger dozed at his feet, a hairy, half grown bundle of a dog, ears twitching at the sound of zaps and lasers as James blasted the alien spaceships flying across his computer screen.

James was glad he had his new computer games. The holidays were not going well. His father had been ill all summer and no one knew why. Although worried about this, his mother had had to visit his aging grandmother. James was happy to help his father, but he was bored and missed his mother. Thank goodness, he thought, for Digger, his four-legged pal.

"Watch out!" called James as Digger suddenly scrambled up, growling and bristling at something in the darkness outside the window. Before boy and dog could move, the lights fizzled and a crackling streak of white blazed through the glass straight into James's computer. James's head turned and his mouth fell open as, with loud beeping, a picture of Scarduggen Castle flashed on to the screen.

"Dad, Dad!" cried James. But his father was asleep in his chair as if nothing had happened. And there was no storm, no sign of anything changed - only the computer, the dark, and a low whimper from Digger. Forgetting the dark, and carefully, very, very carefully, James inspected the machine. "Wish me luck, Dig!" he whispered, reaching slowly for the keyboard. He almost hit the ceiling as, at the touch of his finger, a message appeared on the screen.

"Welcome, James, son of Purbeck!
I thank you for this chance at last to speak.
The Baron's power is strong,
Holding me at Scarduggen five centuries long.
For your father's sake I ask,
Your courage in a brave and daring task."

"There, see, Dig. It was only lightning and this is just a game! Good old Dad must have set it up." His Dad snored on. "Just a game, Digger!" he repeated in a grown-up way and pressed the start key.

But he froze as a man's face flickered onto the screen while a voice curled in a whisper from the computer.

"This be no game!
For your help against the Baron I came!
Your father's ill,
So you must seek the Purbeck ring.
It lies under Scarduggen Castle still.
Find it, but avoid the Baron's sting!"

Somehow the goodness of the tired face filled the room, protecting James. In some mysterious way, through his computer, a ghostly adventure had begun! On the screen there flashed now a picture of a room with a boy, a dog, a lantern and a spade. Then nothing more would change, no matter which keys he pressed. Slowly, James began to understand. He crossed quietly to the kitchen where he found his father's torch. He took the spade from outside the back door, unhooked Digger's lead and pulled on his coat. One touch on the computer keyboard was enough. New instructions appeared before him. Scared but still excited, James copied them down on a scrap of paper. Soon he was ready, shivering with Digger in the cold, still night, a prickliness creeping down his neck. High above in the stony blackness of the tower, two jewel green eyes watched and waited.

"*Between church and tower lies a gate.*
From there move forward, paces eight."

James read from his paper. Swallowing his fear, Digger by his side, he shone the torch over the spiky grass and counted eight steps towards the tower from the ancient gate. But unseen, way above the torchbeam, a velvet black shape crept closer.

James read out the next clue.

"*Wait till moonlight falls*
Upon those dimlit walls,
For there you'll find
Two beasts of different kind."

In the minutes before the moon rose over the castle, James felt his heart thumping. The blackness seemed to thicken beyond the torchlight and an eery mist swirled around his legs. Then, in an instant, the moon was above, it's light pouring down to flood two carvings, a lion and a wolf. James gasped. Shaking, he read the last clue.

"*Looking at each one, place your hand upon it.*
Then take the ring and free my spirit!"

58

As his hands touched the moonlit carvings a great sigh seemed to rush from the ground beneath him, the grass stretching and tearing as a long section began to lift, tilting him towards the tower walls and sending Digger running.

When James dared to look, the air was still again. He saw the raised ground formed a trap door and knew the end of his adventure lay beneath it. Pushing out thoughts of home and comfort, he knelt to pick up his torch. By its light, with a treasure hunter's thrill, he reached for his spade and dug at the soft, brown earth. It was then the black shape leapt from the tower, green eyes gleaming, claws outstretched ready to land with ghostly power upon the ground raised above the boy. The sound of awful laughter made James lift his head and freeze in horror.

Like a bundle of fire, Digger came flying through the air. Brown fur hit black, spinning it away from the trapdoor, pinning it down beneath the tower. A dreadful howl filled the night then stopped suddenly as the phantom cat vanished. James gulped air.

"Digger," he managed to croak. The dog limped over, scraped at the soil and whined. James saw now he'd uncovered a small box. With trembling hands, he lifted it into the moonlight.

"The Purbeck ring!" he cried. The lid turned back to reveal a lovely stone set in gold and there, carved around it, was his family name, Purbeck. "Look, Dig!" he said softly, turning to the dog. But instead of Digger's eyes, there, for an instant, were the eyes from the face that had appeared on his computer screen.

"James, James!" At the shout the boy turned. There was his father ‑ his father running as he hadn't been able to for months! James looked back at his dog. But now it was only Digger, his good and faithful pal. Somehow he knew his strange adventure was over. But more than that, he knew his father's illness was over too. A haunting was ended, the evil of Scarduggen was gone. And what a story he had to tell!

"James, what are you doing?" Mr. Purbeck cried as he reached his son.

"Dad, it's all right. It's finished now! All done! Come and look at this! . . ."

THE END